SAINT NICHOLAS

by Ann Tompert

Illustrated by Michael Garland

Boyds Mills Press

*For librarians, the unsung heroes
and heroines of the literary world*

—A. T.

For my brother, John

—M. G.

Published by Caroline House
Boyds Mills Press, Inc.
A Highlights Company
815 Church Street
Honesdale, Pennsylvania 18431
Printed in China

U.S. Cataloging-in-Publication Data
   (Library of Congress Standards)

Tompert, Ann.
    Saint Nicholas / by Ann Tompert ; illustrated by
Michael Garland.—1st ed.
[32]p. : col. ill. ;   cm.
Summary: A picture book biography of the patron saint of children.
ISBN 1-56397-844-X
1. Nicholas, Saint, Bp. of Myra. 2. Santa Claus. I. Garland, Michael,
ill. II. Title.
270.2/ 092/ 4 [B]—dc21   2000   AC   CIP
99-91821

First edition, 2000
The text of this book is set in 15-point Usherwood Medium.
The illustrations are in mixed media.
Visit us on the World Wide Web at www.boydsmillspress.com

10 9 8 7 6 5 4 3 2 1

Preface

Nearly everyone, it seems, has heard of Santa Claus. But how many know of Saint Nicholas, his historical ancestor?

Much of what we know of Nicholas is derived from the many legends that have come down through the ages. I was somewhat hesitant to write a biography of Nicholas based on legends until I was reminded that legends themselves are generally based on historical facts. These facts are frequently adorned with fanciful, even miraculous, details, added to make the story more interesting.

As an example, we may accept as historical fact that Nicholas rescued some kidnapped boys. There are several versions of how he accomplished this feat. Do the details matter?

What *does* matter is that the story of Nicholas is the story of a man of God who loved his neighbors and was ever ready to help them in any way he could. He was truly a more-than-worthy ancestor of Santa Claus.

—Ann Tompert

NICHOLAS LIVED MORE THAN ONE THOUSAND YEARS AGO in the ancient land of Lycia. He was born around the year 275 and grew up in Patara, a town on the northern coast of the Mediterranean Sea. Now a part of Turkey, the land at that time was part of the Roman Empire.

Nicholas was the only child of elderly parents. His father, Epishanus, and his mother, Joanna, were pious and wealthy landowners, who were widely known for their good deeds.

When Nicholas was about thirteen years old,
his parents died during a plague. His uncle, the
Bishop of Patara, became his guardian.

Nicholas was heir to his parents' fortune and continued their charitable work. He gave food, clothing, and money to the needy.

A well-known story recounts how Nicholas saved a young woman from slavery. Her father, a widowed nobleman, had fallen from riches to poverty. Although his three daughters had many suitors, they could not marry because he was too poor to provide them with the dowry of money or property that a bride was expected to bring to her marriage. The eldest daughter decided to sell herself as a slave in order to raise money for her sisters' dowries.

Nicholas heard about the women's plight. Secretly, in the dark of night, he lowered a small bag of gold through an open window of the eldest daughter's room. With the dowry that Nicholas had provided, she was to able to marry. On two other nights, Nicholas secretly provided the two remaining daughters with dowries of their own.

Because of such good work, Nicholas eventually became the patron of young women seeking husbands. Some paintings show Nicholas holding three gold balls, which represent the three bags of gold.

Under his uncle's guidance, Nicholas studied for the priesthood. He assisted at baptisms, weddings, and funerals. He visited the sick, carrying baskets of food and medicines. He was such a diligent and devout student that he became a priest when he was only nineteen.

Soon after, his uncle the bishop went on a pilgrimage to Jerusalem, leaving Nicholas in charge of his congregation. Nicholas is said to have cared for the church's people as well as did the bishop himself.

When his uncle came home, Nicholas made his own pilgrimage to Jerusalem. He visited many sacred places in the Holy Land, walking in the steps of the first Christians. Suddenly, he felt an overwhelming urge to return to Lycia.

Nicholas hurried to the nearest port. He boarded a ship and set sail. When the ship reached the middle of the Mediterranean Sea, the sky exploded with lightning and thunder. A violent wind shredded the sails and snapped the main mast. Forty-foot-high waves tossed the ship about like a cork. The terrified sailors begged Nicholas to pray for their safety. For two days and two nights, wind and water battered the ship. For two days and two nights, Nicholas prayed that he and the crew would be delivered from the angry sea.

Early on the third morning, the storm passed. The sailors thanked Nicholas for protecting them from the tempest. When the sky cleared, they were surprised to find themselves near the safe harbor at Myra, a city near Patara, Nicholas's home. Word of how Nicholas had calmed the storm began to spread. Soon he was considered the patron of sailors.

From the shores of Myra, Nicholas walked three miles to the cathedral. He wished to give thanks to God for delivering the ship from the storm. When he approached the church, a priest asked him his name. Learning that it was Nicholas, the priest was overjoyed. Nicholas was bewildered.

The priest explained that the people had been seeking a bishop to succeed the bishop who had died. In a dream, the priest had heard a voice tell him to stand near the door of the cathedral, where he was to wait for the first man named Nicholas. That man, said the voice, would be the new bishop of Myra. Nicholas protested that he was not worthy. But soon he was wearing the bishop's miter on his head, holding the bishop's crosier in his hand, and sitting in the bishop's chair.

Although he was called the "Boy Bishop" because of his youth, the people of Myra and all Lycia loved and respected him. One early legend relates how Nicholas helped the people.

Bad weather had caused a great shortage of food in Lycia. Fear of famine stalked the land. While Nicholas was trying desperately to find grain for the people, he heard that several ships had anchored in the port of Myra. The ships were carrying grain from Egypt to Constantinople.

Nicholas hurried to the harbor and urged the ships' captains to set aside some of their grain for the hungry of Lycia. At first, the captains refused, saying they would be held responsible for any shortages. But Nicholas assured them there would be no shortage of grain. The captains set aside one hundred bushels of wheat from each ship. When the ships reached Constantinople, the cargo weighed exactly what it had when the ships left Egypt.

Another legend about the young bishop tells of three schoolboys traveling home from boarding school for the holidays. They stopped overnight at an inn, where a villainous innkeeper held them for ransom. The boys' distraught parents asked Nicholas for help.

Nicholas searched the road until he discovered the inn. There, the innkeeper admitted he had butchered the boys and put their remains into pickling barrels. Nicholas waved his crosier. The boys stepped from the barrels, alive and well. Because of this miracle, Nicholas became the patron of students and of all children.

When Nicholas was in his twenties, the Roman emperor, Diocletian, demanded that all Roman citizens worship him as a god. Bishop Nicholas and his congregation, like many Christians, refused to obey the order. Roman soldiers destroyed the churches and burned their sacred books. "Churches may fall," said Nicholas, "but Christians must stand." He and his congregation were thrown into prison.

For ten long years, they suffered cold, hunger, and thirst. Then Rome crowned a new ruler—Constantine, the first Roman emperor to convert to Christianity. Constantine freed all Christians from prison, and Nicholas returned as Bishop of Myra.

Nicholas spent the rest of his life as a beloved leader, converting people to Christianity and helping the poor and needy. By the time of his death on December 6, 343, stories of his good deeds and miracles had spread throughout Lycia and beyond. In time, the boy Nicholas of Patara was declared Saint Nicholas of Myra.

Author's Note

Even before his death, sailors adopted Nicholas as their patron. Boatmen sailing on the rivers of Europe spread word of their patron and his miraculous deeds. Others took him as their patron as well: fishermen, wood-turners, cobblers, tailors, bakers, shopkeepers, and students, among them.

In 1087, when war ravished Lycia, devotees of Nicholas, fearing his remains would be desecrated by marauding armies, stealthily removed them from Myra to Bari, Italy. Biographies, poems, and plays were written about Nicholas during the Middle Ages. Hundreds of hymns were composed in his honor. Statues, paintings, and stained-glass windows depicted the legends of his life. By the fifteenth century, close to two thousand chapels, hospitals, and monasteries had been named after him.

As early as the twelfth century, Saint Nicholas was credited with giving gifts to good children on the eve of his feast day, December 6. He left them in shoes, stockings, and paper boats that were set out for that purpose.

Through the following centuries, gift-giving customs changed. The day was moved to Christmas Eve, New Year's Day, or January 5, the eve of the Epiphany. The gift-giver's appearance changed, too. He came to be known by different names, among them Kris Kringle, Father Christmas, and Grandfather Frost.

The people of Holland still acknowledge Saint Nicholas, whom they call Sinterklass. In the seventeenth century, they brought the legend with them when they settled in what is now the state of New York. Some historians claim that Santa Claus is a descendent of the Saint Nicholas of the Dutch. Others disagree, claiming that the Santa Claus of today is the invention of three Americans: writer Washington Irving, who introduced him in his humorous book *Diedrich Knickerbocker's A History of New York*; educator Clement Moore, who brought him to life in his "A Visit from St. Nicholas;" and cartoonist Thomas Nast, who added the visual dimension.

We may never know the true story. We do know, however, that Santa Claus retains the essential feature of Saint Nicholas as the giver of gifts. I like to think that somehow they share the same family tree.